Other books by, Mr. Rodney Paul Banks

Even Shorter Stories I

Even Shorter Stories II

Even Shorter Stories III

Rodney Paul Williams

authorHOUSE®

AuthorHouse™
1663 Liberty Drive
Bloomington, IN 47403
www.authorhouse.com
Phone: 833-262-8899

Published by AuthorHouse 07/13/2022

ISBN: 978-1-6655-6505-9 (sc)
ISBN: 978-1-6655-6504-2 (e)

Print information available on the last page.

This book is printed on acid-free paper.

CONTENTS

ATTITUDE ADJUSTMENT NEEDED

Her children drive me nuts. Meryl and I have been together for over 8 months new. Meryl his six sharp girls aged between three years one month and one day. She you answer one in exactly that way depending on the date and time of day. Believe me she is aware of the exact time of night she popped out. She will tell you the hour(s) and minute(s) of her age and is never inaccurate. I have to come to know.

We were for instance let me tell you in the restaurant on Thanksgiving Day Chiffs, the seven-year old mid-Scorpio pointed discriminately to her older brother Joshua's shirt front. He had spilled a drip or two soy sauce from his Beef and noodles with gravy with broccoli and tomatoes. I called the Cho Lai, the Vietnamese waitress and Joshua, requested in his own words. "Please Mrs. Cho Lai, will be bring to me the proper solution in order that I may unsoil, showing the waitress his mishap, light blue shirts button and placket. We are doing a short scientific experiment–photos before and after we dine. Mom could possible embarrassed if I am too disorderly after the meal."

Cho Lai smiled inscrutably. Yes, I know inscrutable is normally associated with the Japanese tradition and heritage, but in my mind, I have to get back at her in some way. I know behind her inscrutable smile is the pure awareness of a much larger tip. The extra service and bright atmospheric personalities we always have received deserves the accredited tips plus extra. I am always satisfied. Meryl, the children and I satisfied ourselves with the food's flavors.

Happy Halloween

The entire planet celebrating the one-year anniversary. Every major power is now fully rebuilt. Today is Halloween one-year later.

The planet again shutters. A meteor has landed. An extremely big one. Breathes are held. People around the planet barely doubt. Fears on all fronts rise.

It started in this way one year ago this night. The trick or treating was over. Rader showed two more meteor like objects fastly approaching. Their paths leading to direct contact. Now with the confirmation of the approaching projectiles alerts Earth-wide sounded. This time we will be ready.

It had taken hours the last time for the spaceships melted earth to cool and the Martian's ships to appear out of the sand, rock and dirt.

Each government ordered of biological deceases and spore like germs to use in mankind's defense.

All concerned convinced that the germs would save mankind again were to prove in seven days from the multiple tri-landings countries over the space of this planet proved correct.

On day three of the Martian invasion plans were being directed to engineers on Earth rebuilding. As the prior invasion this invasion would cause major reconstruction of homes, businesses, and highways. This now being known rebuilding would take less than six months by the planning commissions estimates. The account would have been.

In seven days, the alien ships fell from the skies. The same as last year. In seven days, the aliens died off. The same as last year. In seven days, those microscopic Earthlings killed the Martians.

There was not one difference this year. After seven days on the eighth day when rebuilding was scheduled to begin giving the re-order of life an educated resorts and asteroid landed in Sand Bernadino, California. Then two more landed within a quarter qulometer of the first and around the planet tri-landings.

The Martians had been educated.

20-20

The quick flash of blue light was succeeded by black and white lights side by side cloudy with curly edges. And awakening to the idea his plan he had put over it Wonder lasted a short moment. The inquiring lasted but a second or two of time. Is this my black eye. The wonderment ended and clarity no longer had eluded him. Successfully he closed out be conscience at all but the most minute part of a fraction of a second. Blocking the thought of losing that eye from consciousness. That time came to end fifty years later. Watching the movie, it the thought of being one eye short just emptied itself in his now conscious brain. He started writing a short monument to God's creations stability and endurance.

WIDE EYED MOM

The weather changed its course of sections quickly. Seventy degrees one week throughout. Two days later ninety degree days and eighty degree evening, caused me to sweat for the first time in years. The first day on the preciface of a weeklong heatwave. That, if you may allow to swept the weeklong term as the normal fire days, work-week Monday to Friday.

Thank God there is air conditioning.

She pulls off her tanker, her shorts and her panties. The early part of the day she had decided was too muggy to wear a bra. Madgette, her three-year-old reached for her thong line to assist in the disrobing. Just as she reached her mother not anticipating the gesture, bent over while pulling her G string and Madgette's fingers easily accidently inserted.

Titan's Reverse Orbit

Not yet being able to figure out their language by the glyphs, I found in the debris, it took me somewhile to figure it. Once getting a gander on the solution it all fell directly on my path conception.

I has been almost fifty years since the angina come into the telescopes of our big brained astrological geniuses and I turn out to be their enlightener.

Doctor degrees attached themselves to males and females. More than one thousand members of The Outer Space Astrological Society with dual doctorates locked in on future space travel saw it could not figure how this possibility attributed its actuality. Deciding to bypass what was right there in-front of their eyes in our own solar system all but one of those most educated in their field gave up on the road to solving the problem which crossed each of blackboard.

I have twelve credits towards my own college associate degree. Those I have are in communications geared towards entertainments developing the stage materials to lend actors and ease to show off their mobil and verbal skills.

In other words, my discovery -totally lucky. Titan the large satellite circling Jupiter was at one time a part of a living being and it is still bleeding.

I know the simplest thing shot down the bigwig brains of theirs. Contrastingly what stumped them gave me the answer. They got stuck on the fact that the then planet rotated in a different direction than did its moon. To me it was obvious a force had to put Titan the moon in a reverse orbit than the then planet it rotated about.

The truth showed in my brain as clear as a home movie. A three-way extraterrestrial love affair caused it. The three participants must have been enormous. The fight between the two males ended with the explosion of winner's weapon hit what we call Titan in his back and shattered him as pieces of glass while Titan was running away from a pure cause of a serious can of ass whip being opened on him. That piece we call the moon of Titan got caught in Jupiter's gravity while passing the ex planet. Thus, the reverse orbit. Easy.

WRITER'S _ _ _ _ HEAD

I jut get rid of it. It had happened to me before. Two other times. Once in nineteen seventy-nine when lost my college story on the city mayor. I also lost my other story I wrote. The Fear. In the early part of two thousand, I fell asleep on the overail train. I awoke surprised quickly got off the public conveyance at my stop. I left my book. Both times I had it.

This time, I have backups. So, what if my three Xerox copies are in my Westside as is my original handwritten one.

Oh shit! I wanted to think son of a damned bitch, but no puppy I know of deserves that curse. That is unless some human being went against that little block bestselling book with the silver or gold bold letter. I already forgot what I wanted to put down.

This is in the same field as brain freeze. Just a little something something that comes to me unasked for and unwanted. Soon as it does, I want to get rid of it. Writer's block has lasted me a little longer though.

Perhaps I can get away with the probability of a short version of The Correct. I grew in Productive Sail. I would even though that despicable rabbit got serious sick and died when the black duck fed it to him.

Could I steal someone else's idea and parody it? The cartoon South Park is the perfect would-be victim. They [sts or] borrow parody quite often. Guess there are no complains. They most often do excellent work when pitch or borrow.

ARREST AND TRIAL VS. LAW AND ORDER

Cholo Garcia first lieutenant of the Red Rattlesnake an upper middle class Brazilian Portuguese group of young adult contract assassins walked into his center city one million three hundred thousand condominium. There were two stories above the floor his home in the thirty-one-story condo complex. As his electronic key security door closed and locked his contract with Retail Sales Realty activated. Secured he bit his knees on a four-inch-thick Chinese handmade rug lied down on his floor and rolled over the room over and over with hilarious body gestures and gregariously laughing.

Half an hour earlier, him I know, said the homicide detective to arrest superior officer. They stopped, Cholo had a little conversation. Asking Cholo to give up info, fishing actually hoping to get anything they could. To no avail the first officer affectionately put on Cholo's shoulders as though the two were old friends. His superior to the snapshot photo and gave that old threat that they would pass it around Cholo's crew members.

When Cholo walked away he knew his people were going to do the same as he would soon be doing. Just that week his people were watching that same scene but on the daily T.V. show Arrest and Trial.

That police ploy had played out. The real comedy was the police unlike criminals even the criminals in the correctional institutionalized prison's without fail watched every show about police. The joke is on the police.

Two days later, Cholo Garcia's intelligence proved totally correct.

THE ZIL

Cycollphe, it was discovered was for a short time less than a year on Earth was at war with Zil. Zil a solar system of sentient beings completely destroyed all that existed of Cycollphe including the atmosphere and the lack of atmosphere. This the war between the two worlds where Zil had been without cause infiltrated and invaded. The vestige of Cycollphe was a special conveyance attempting to escape their genocide.

The Zil warship that had the priviledge of ending their antagonist returned home.

Ten thousand Earth years later a few minor pieces of the invader's conveyance drifted into Earth's orbital atmosphere. Thirty years later technology from that debris inundated Human machines.

From a trillion miles of firmament away that technology was now in so much use. Zil technology detected the insult.

The Zil onslaught was so fast and its devastation complete, not only did complete that no presence of Earth's existence ever again be recorded by alien visitors Earth's recordings from outer space beings billions of light years away from where the blue marble used to be negated it from their own historical archives.

NEXT STOP–PHYSICAL THERAPY

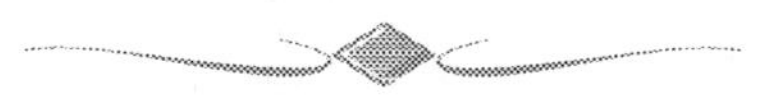

The tens electrical muscle stimulator now finished its purpose for this visit Doctor Ried's patient continuous his conversation. He as usual has been very wordy. His words seem to be and or actually are very welcome. His conversations have always during his appointments have been developed, interesting and a testament to stimulating conversations. Not most but off times informational. Today he conversed about the second shooter who had been on the tapes of the assassination of President John Fitzgerald Kennedy, who had fought for human rights of rights of the negroid Americans more than any Caucasian in the history of the U. S.

Somehow the conversation forwarded itself from R. P. Banks, the patient to the female sex.

During that part of their verbal complementary exchange Banks noted the almost two hundred handwritten pages of his new book in his backpack he wanted the doctor's partner to read. His partner & published author already.

Banks explained this writing was of fictitious work, mostly. He had all but verbally stumbled trying to remember the word fiction.

To bring some levity into his conversation while leaving, he stated this one was on how all the short stories her were dedicated to the point that all the women loved him.

All in the front of the office were cordially amused and laughing as he made his way through door towards the elevator sign. Him too twelfth floor.

The Selection

His success was greeted with three straight weekends at earning the most box office case. In the weeks since opening three quartet billion dollars was grossed. The fourth week, Mickey Galactic and his Scary Commandos eased him into a second place.

He was interviewed by Lois Lang the highest paid magazine interviewers for the lost decade. Of all the producers, writers, actors, and political geniuses she was more wordly recognized. Pre-school children knew her name, face and even her voice inflections at first sound and at first sight.

The questions she had put down to bring up to him were answered eloquently with the Kindness of lightheartedness one could expect and all were gone over on his first soliloquy. She had no query for him soon after she said hello.

The magazines story went so well she would overtake the leader of the Sara Palsey Award leader for that year, sad win it, the only writer's award that had [cloded] her in the most illustrious career of all time even in the distant future.

He was offered and earned parts in the eleven top advertised global projects in his field. Guess starring, co-starting and Special Guess Starring in them all. H chose not to star so his time would allow him to become the new most famous name and face on the planet. He earned that all from the films from his starring role in Mickey Galactic his first appearance on screen. The only thing in his mind at the hang interview was what was on his mind since he had been signed for the lead was that he had beaten \\ lhon Jayne, the greatest action actor of all time.

For the Oscars he won the thing in Jest, winning against the part of a hoodlum in Mars in small potatoes and the part of Blue E. in the film Melissa's rapist. Those were the only the nominees for costart and he portrayed the winning one overshadowing his other two nominated parts.

Knowing his future was now solidly secure he gave his sole interview on winning the award to upstart radio co-anchor and middle-weight weightlifting champion whose parents had refused to chose a sexual orientation when their healthy bouncing newborn broke out of the nine month water park, road down the water slide and kissed the waiting obstetricians awaiting hands. The sole reason Mickey chose this inquisitor is both organs were widely known to still be were they all ways were Courage.

Flip'd the Tip

The Late Night Show with host, Samien Sine is the number watched weeknight television talk show of all time, second only to the weekday evening news programs and it took three different news station shows to heat his [xxx] viewing number and viewer ratings. On the night you go on Sine's show will crush them. All of them.

Byrney Baxter Merridith heard the agent representing the show of all the Glamour Magazine over the past half year.

Merridith is a hermaphrodite recently having successful sex surgery transplanting the penial part of the sexual organ from the it was since birth. The idea came to Merridith in a flash at an epiphany.

Sex life had [run the ring] of the ladder men, women, both at the same time but, even though every style and every position tried equaled and surpassed those in the book of Kama Sutra. [xxx] was sort of [xxx] when the missionary position was instituted and that was very often since she and Mya, another dual sexed one moved in her thirty room, nine-bedroom thirteen bath with the main bedroom and main two [xxx] bedroom eight-foot-long tubs.

Her operation, which was the epiphany took she and Mya to heights no dual sex organed human had ever done nor had any ever before felt.

It seemed that nature had decided to eliminate the number of born hermaphrodites at the least make their numbers more difficult to advance. All hermaphrodites were born in, you can picture them with their testacle inside the body, but more inefficiently for rebirth their penises above their vagina.

Byrney Baxter Merridith's flash idea was the operation. Move the penis of either of the couple from stop the vagina to below the vagina. Keeping everything working the two non- fit lit in glove both ways.

Mya will not be as famous as long as you. Byrney will be on the show too. "And I got you the final spot on the s[x] with fifteen spare minutes should anyone's time run a little over." Meredith's manager continued.

With his one diamond tooth smile naturally, she stole a line from other television shows in a case as this, asking "Who's the greatest manager?"

One Moved Ahead Better

Lights came on in Gadenske, New Zealand, at eight zero one p.m. exactly as scheduled as they have done so in the past two decades plus nine years. The exact happened to every light in the time zone.

Visiting after delaying their family vacation for health reasons were Blackstone Ojee and his family. Maria, his wife, just over an oddity feeling her womanliness finally plugged.

It had been running full stream thirty-two days stopping four days prior to the vacation start.

At the touching of the corporate jet's tires Blackstone's whole view of this vacation had changed to sheer awareness. There must have been something horrifyingly wrong.

His usually tacit visage had turned to a [xxx] of calm enjoying effervescent contentedness. His family finally back on the land of their births brought them solemnity of rejoice. Then the tire breaks began on to validation.

The Miracle slammed on the breaks of contented peacefulness, and he became fully knowledgeable. He had become aware. A heavy full tear continued down it's [frock.]

The plan to reverse the damage of time, only the ending had he envisioned.

With that in mind a thin line of bewilderment come accompanying the lightly furrowed brow acknowledging his ex-wife's achievement.

Damn be contemplated now that he had realized she must go and done it. Now how to disrupt be accomplishment and thwart that arrogant grin most likely addressing that pimply little face with the lumberjack square chin.

He at that could not have realized, she decades pass had completely decided to forget him completely and she had done so very successfully. The only arrogance between the two of there was his own.

[Advertisingly] as she had become accustomed to was in her own most feminine way hooting, howling, and salaciously with spittle drizzling down both her cheeks towards her soaked to a mat whitening crown of glory moaning so the entire sky scraper with no doubts allowed her pleasure to be known both legs about to drop to the hundred year old pear and pomegranate pattern Persian two in thick plush carpet, the other to the wide cashmere covered couch extra wide for her long legged seven foot three inch boy toy, Diogenes Alegando Zacks.

Soon she clumped to it out cold.

In Your Face

"Dude!! What the heck is wrong with you? You bought those cookies from that guy."

"Sure, I did. I got half dozen Tell me you did not! That is the same guy who came here only a couple of weeks ago. Remember! You took some home to Sarah. You do remember Sarah, your wife, eight months pregnant. The last time you paid him for some of those cookies was right here on this same spot. That same guy. You got serious food poisoning. Sarah almost died!! Remember Sarah, your almost dead pregnant wife and almost killed the two of your unborn child? As soon as you saw him come here you should have cracked his skull, stomped him and then had him arrested!! I cannot believe he just walked away from here! Unscathed!!"

"You dumb, idiotic punk-ass-son-of-a-bitch!! I hope Sarah finds out!"

This story was written on cookies. The truth is here's what the story is about, Pimps prostitutes, STD's and the tricks seeing the Pimp come back to where he forced the prostitute to sell herself while knowing she was infectious with chlamydia and returning to the tricks job again and leaving unharmed.

I Know What I Would Think

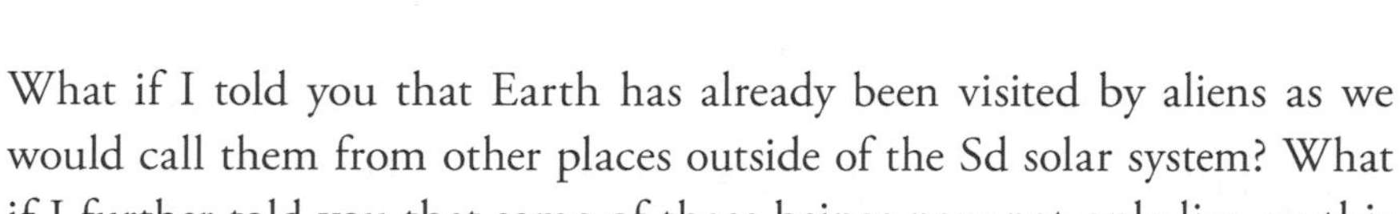

What if I told you that Earth has already been visited by aliens as we would call them from other places outside of the Sd solar system? What if I further told you that some of those beings now not only live on this planet but have also colonized it?

What if I told you in colonizing Earth the others have changed things to suit their home world platitudes? What if I told you that those intruders do not recognize human beings? What did I tell you that all living and non-living things here are now only cared for but used every day by those beings? What if I told you that mostly every other life forms out there recognize the beings as being the true dominant inhabitants of this place known to us by various names? What if those alternate beings' co habit now on this ball and have established trade routes both to and from here? \\!hat if I told you the fowl, animals, plants and preside are staples as is grain and air? What if I told you that those beings have established ways of travel on this place and make daily use of them air, land sea and osmosis? What if I told you that the outer spacers cannot even physically interview by sound nor by touch nor via any other means? We simply put do not exist to them. I tell you this without what if? What if I looked you directly in your eyes and you could not see me? What if I told you every day and every night you look them in their eyes and do not see them nor do you see their world? What would you think if I told you? It is force.

Rodney Banks to Rodney Sterling

W'ith the shows on werewolves and vampires today, I would like to ascertain how you accepted your twilight zone.

[SEEEE]

I wonder why no writer ever gives Mrs. Godzilla her true props really no probs at all. I understand even if others do not. A movie has been written, directed, acted, and filmed with Godzilla, Godzilla's son. He came about, somehow. Add to that the fact even before Godzuki, which continues in every Godzilla movie his immaculate manicures and pedicures.

Tall Tales

In my lifetime the truth has been shall we say stretched a might.

The most I have ever really knew the lie was the day former president number thirty-seven was said to be a liar. The stretch here was that for some reason, no one else was. Or should it be written that everyone else in the government must have only said truths.

Most of us of my age remember the other deep throat. That twelve-inch swallow job cheerly shows the one-foot ruler doing the measuring started the reading of the twelve inches at close to three inches and still had an inch may be an inch and a half left above the tip.

Families were compared of a father, a mother, and children. Some viewed the tell the truth signs boasting that a lie. i.e., three things' children do not believe in: Santa Claus, The Easter Bunny, and fathers. Father's [xxx] their own children? [Poh lease.]

Here is an op to date one, Cosby is a rapist. Oh [xxx] oh remember this on 0.J. did it.

The police job is to ''Protest and to Serve''.

Students always are aware of the famous colleges they attend's background. It took me nine years to have Penn State answer this question correctly, what does the word Nittany means in the title Nittany Lions.

Television personalities are all always stand up, loyal and honest people. Someone should give all those employed by Walt Disney polygraphs.

Everyone wants to be told bad news about people-other people. If this is so, re-read the statement above.

Enough said, for the present, you look.

For the People

Aragua, Venezuela, and Brazil planned it to the utmost of transcendence. Their former predatory adversary would be no more than one year. The United States of America was at this very moment not only so severely wounded to the point of hemorrhaging, but she is fallen and cannot get up. And entire three fifth of the land mass was in radioactive flams. Alabama, Alaska, California, Colorado, Delaware, Florida, Iowa, New Hampshire, New York, Ohio, Pennsylvania, and Washington, all had within one minute of each other had two to six hydrogen bombs exploded in them. Two bombs to each of the smaller states on upward in number to six in the largest states.

The plan started some sixteen years earlier. Punk-ass took a two-year-old child from a woman in an urban city while forcing her into slavery-human trafficking. As the legal authorities had done with a former kidnapper-rapist-human trafficker, Gary Heidrick, nothing until one of his captives escaped and told of the Heidrick basement dungeon.

People including family members of the victims had reported to the police that female family members turned up missing for about a couple of year. No investigations were initiated possibly due to the missing being poor in money and prostitutes on the streets.

Although this particular boy went off the grid the Federal Bureau of Investigation. The Special Victims Unit, The Cities Mayor and police gave no investigation on the boy, the mother, nor the woman's fourteen-year-old daughter.

Here the South American drug cartel's saw a huge weakness in the U. S. A. and decided that their imprisoned and their dead Cape's chance for revenge had a high percentage of success.

Japan, Vietnam, Korea, Ghana, Namibia, Senegal were all enlisted to purchase the nuclear materials. The later three were hardly spied on by the U. S. The U. S, hierarchy thought themselves and the U.S. government safe from them due to the U.S's complicity in the Apartheid movement of South Africa.

Mexico, Guatemala, Puerto Rico, and the Dominican Republic supplied people and vehicles along with safe houses because in the aftermath those peoples would gain land and prominence.

No Caucasian nor black American whose family ties had been in their country since before slavery and near that timespan of two hundred years were considered as what could conscript, except that child ripped from his engraved, human trafficked mother and at the time of his remover fourteen year-old sister. The two females though held more than nine years got the call to enlist in the bombings.

Less than three weeks later armed convoys from Germany, Japan, Czechoslovakia, Russia and China. The U. S's, end came.

THE ENDING IS GOOD

Thomas Jonah Meatland finally smiled once ensconced in the driver's seat of his white and burgundy Bentley Continental G.T. He had no reason to smile for some years. The woman the former Mrs. Sarahi Meatland had chested on him over nine years finally divorcing him for her present-day husband Robert D. Niro Smith, a coffee baron.

His uncomfortable stature having improved only over the last couple of moments come according to more than six hundred thousand of his most prime Hereford and Angus steer being fed upon by [sangvivores.] The bats were difficult at the least to be rid of. The epidemics attacked over and over seemingly without cessation. The mammals' tongues nearly drank the rancher into bankruptcy. Then for some reason the feedings stopped.

Most of his cattle had been drank to death. The guards hired to ward them off were thwarted by the vastness in plethora of numbers. Zoologists hired explained the oddity of the bats flying to and from the hoards. Normally the vampire bats hopped on the group to stealthily attack their prey. The other strongness, the feeders aggravated the steers. Meatland was told by the scientist that, that type of bat most often fed on its' prey without the prey even being the slightest way aware. The great numbers changed that completely. Cattle as earlier stated died from them being fed upon by so many of one time.

One week for some miracle or another the [sanguinores] vanished.

"Hi T." she said, "How about a lift?" Thomas had met this female over three years ago. They had hit it off. She was in the process of divorcing then, so nothing other than a Pabst Blue Ribbon beer exchanged between them, other than phone numbers, addresses and good wishes.

The woman was wealthy, and the spitting image of her mother Marilyn.

After a couple of words, smiles and very short, timed daydream aspirations, Jenny Monroe got in.

In doing so, he could see the pink thong through her sheerest of micromini sundress. They traversed.

THE PANTIES THREE

Absolutely [xxx] lately kept, windows lawns, shrubs, carpets, rugs, furniture everything.

Live in housekeepers, cooks, gardeners, chauffeurs, cooks, the while sooner. There were three live in buildings for the hired help. All were on the same [acologe] separated from the main house.

The two United States Marine Officers had left her a moment or two ago. In such units as the ones the Marines were assigned as their detail news was never good.

Her only relative Lieutenant Colonel was a killed in action in Central Afghanistan. Today was September twelfth two thousand eleven.

Up and coming actor Ulik Mole her would have been future life partner without her knowing had last week signed a half billion dollar acting contract. Four days ago, he moved out.

The news Lashley Tech was not going public with their stock gave her some news. The tip given her the new stock was about to be a disrupter putting all other biotech stocks in the long-distance rear-view mirror.

Distraught had never before crossed her demeaner. It had never before shadowed her countenance until she entered her eight-car garage. She chose the twenty twenty three Couette C ten.

The doors opened and closed automatically.

Shortly before a half hour passes she stops near the bridge center exits her automobile, climbs the rail and jumps.

Luckily a Bridge Port Authority Policeman sees her every move, Eagle eyes lock on the stopped Yellow C ten. The hands assigned to those eagle eyes ignites the patrol car as the driver exits the Chevy [Sereeling] breaks do not muffle the radio call. Out jumps the officer, Up and over the guard rails after the C Ten driver.

Television, radio, newspapers go absolutely appreciative to the two [xxx], but nowhere the adoration of the internet. One point six billion hits in less than forty-eight hours.

Civilian Stingray driver and Port Authority officer save life of drawing fourteen year old Asian girl whose water motor cycle malfunctioned and flipped over at eighty miles an hour on Bloose Lake.

Do not pick on me about the title. I am passing this one off on those members of thew news regune.

Silvermaine

Back on American soil the seven-twenty-seven opened its passenger door. The Central Intelligence Agents of the seven entrusted to deliver the prisoner Silvermaine extradited to frame charges of multiple slaughters of mutilations and murders received their orders to allow his departure. Exiting the door shackles in tungsten stainless steel anklets and each wrist in the material wristlets, one to each side of a brand-new waist belt, designed with tungsten steel two-inch-long one-half inch chain attached to each of the belt's sides holding the cuffs tightly to the criminal's sides. The very first stop downward on the aluminum stairs, leading from the jet the ground was the last step he touches on this journey. His head forcefully jerked backward and leftward. He dropped his arm still held by the force C. I. A. agent he crumpled backwards into the transport.

His only relative one quarter mile distant felt relief. His grandfather would never be disgraced with prison doors, bars and walls.

The Right Stuff

Favors, large favors had been done by the newest nightly show host. His show an entire hour in length had already had the latest three Oscar Winner, Star, supporting star and writer. His first week interviewing the first, yet only female president of the Soviet Union. His interview portion of the show tonight aired the Ku Klux Klan's to date only Woman Grand Dragon sure to get an enormous amount and long-lasting call-in and write in response. The Dragon was one of only two guests. The other was the heiress to her father's eleven-billion-dollar fortune. Of the deceased, four children she was third in the line of birth took her other siblings to court over the fortune. Their parents unexpectedly died in the last Bogato Columbian drug lord war. She must have been highly intelligent for no will left an all-out war which she won the courts. Even winning in the Supreme Court trial.

Lawyers who represented the two sons and the eldest a daughter fell before her representation. She represented her own self.

Rodney Paul Banks, after his show thanked his wife Betty for again giving him guest that again put the show's ratings in the top spot across the country.

His amazement with her work proved her the master booker of all time.

On their home his hand being accepted between uppermost thighs, as usually. She inquired and for but the briefest of time almost wished she had not, how he enjoyed his birthday present. Last night, Halloween and his seventieth birthday. He did not quiet get it. He could not think of any present that he had been aware of.

You know you have asked me for decades to meet a hermaphrodite and you just interviewed one.

Worth ... Ahhh ... About to be moist. Their chauffer already knew never to interrupt them while in the rear seating of the Hig Tine model of their Volks Wagon Stretched limo.

FINGER

In the old Datsun 310 two plain clothed police officers were in a third hour of a jewelry heist strikeout. The heist was slow to take place.

Corporal Likt Ismokzw rather than leave the car to relieve himself took his mind off the thought questioned his partner Detective Illi Seth. A Bangladesh hottie in a micro mini perhaps a Tap too Mini Mao. Her palm resting between her open thin legs covering her vagina protruding out of the left side of her clear colored thong. Decided to ask, "do you want to hear a dirty joke?" Her partner only needed his mind off of setting out of the car acquired swiftly.

Set said to him, "Smell this."

QUESTIONABLE

Transpose College, Yorifk, Finland

"Professor, I'd like to gratefully accept this position. Fits into my personality like a worm in a Robbin's beak." The position referred to be the grant given to the school by the U. S. S. R. The Soviet's were tied down to more political [xxx] research to study phrase Commonality in Relation to Authentic Living Practices, so the start.

Starting off contacting N. A. S. A. in the United States of America, the student to attempt retrieval of his life-long [xxx] - the answer, is it really shorter returning than going. He chose to inquire the time it took for the launching to the and landing on the moon opposed to the time it took from lunar departure to the capsule splashing down. There was a substantial difference.

His professor sent his finding on the U. S. A's lunar launching along with some one hundred and one other data findings. The answer to the ad age the student surpasses the teacher does remain a query. The Soviet shut down the grant immediately.

CONSISTENCY

Fifty year old Sagittarius Herman Aster Lentz being a devout Hebrew has been blessed today by God whose name is jealous.

His heart has cried aloud for the last eleven years three months and day and a [hat]. His mouth be kept silent.

Only the idea of his to, Chelot Vix.

Boler, that a recent widow should not be punished with chastity for even one day or night had she been monogamous to her deceased mate while trained.

On this day October 31", 1953, he sleeps co-habitually with the women he has.

Thunderously argued in his chest against his loins a [inch) are no longer chastity bound.

For Chelot, she mourns in bliss.

Bliss

Seeing his time was short than Michael Moores, Lucifer began to worry. God had slipped-up and allowed him to see the part of the future that he feared. He would not to be able to bare it even for a second. Eternity glanced him in his face, thought reality shoved the vision in only his thoughts.

He began to do good deeds. Poss out positive advice. During these few minutes one would.

JEALOUS

JEALOUS, I almost wish it weren't true Mayim Birlyk, who hosting & show on television. I have never seen bad, or talked to her in person. I like her even still. Mayim is a married woman with young children. Yet I still like her. The television show she had been, by the time you read this, hosting was the reason for the television commercial.

JEALOUS, I almost wish it weren't true where this idea took birth in my head. You're hot. I now you're married, but if you can think you've divorced, your husband for a few moments than maybe I can have you and you can have your way with me. Then you mentally remarry him and he'll never know. You will be spoiled.

JEALOUS, I almost wish it weren't true, but only for a little while. All religious criteria met.

HOOONNN! WHEN DID YOU GET 3 BOYFRIENDS???

Ted or rather Theodore Litzske had taken notice

Tediya Litzske his eleven-year-old Scorpio daughter whom a short while ago had stopped letting Ports Smith, the family fully grown Great Done lick her in her face. He noted she instead of closing her eyes and lighted up that broad sunshine super warming smile of hers. It bothered him. She had since she was two years old loved and could hardly wait to allow that licking as soon as she would enter through the home front door.

He had just a short while ago in his Manhattan Exec, Vice Chairman's Office been shown a pornographic video of his company's dose competitor's Chief exec officer's girlfriend with a horse, a hog and a Labrador. To say the lest his mind was on the outer side of the brink of turmoil he fought & won inside himself to deny acceptance of the idea in his trying strenuously not to heart allowing in acceptance.

His fear was eased but only eased as her opened Todiya's bedroom door in hopes of an easy discussion -not on the possible matter with directness. A trait not in his filed of life matter handling.

His daughter he found asleep but talking to herself.

"You had to breakup with me you son-of-a-bitch. I had imagined you finally sneaking into this room after you met my folks.

I envisioned getting my juice broke off Ports Smith. When he could have licked all over my face after he met you and licked my juice off your face. You dirty son-of-a-bitch."

Ted Litzske, silently closed her bedroom door, and as he head up and shoulders back his and his wife's Veztz's get shack his relief building a snow covered mountain along with a not too silent deep breath of relief not hearing his loved daddy's little girl not while still asleep.

"I hope you drown in the South Ocean!! Slowly!!! Until.."

Your Intel

Now that every suspicion on our demise has been rendered unnecessary.

Thirteen years ago, there were thirteen planets the solar system. When an extraordinary occurrence hid the disappear and of the generally unknown Ceres, Hames, Makemake and Eris. Pluto was downgraded from planet status due to Pluto not fitting planet requirement.

Your Intel:

One that same moment Hubble the most recognized space telescope had its weather alert The International Astronomical Union (IAU) that four of the planets orbiting Sol had suddenly disappeared from view.

This phenomenal occurrence could not be covered up by the governments from the major stellar observers, so within one year every earthling had become aware.

When that news had finally been generally excepted, the downrated Pluto to be now called a dwarf disappeared from the firmament.

Exactly one year to that night later Neptune, Pluto's nearest neighbor vanished.

In Neptune's place the same as Pluto was firmament. Neptune upon its unsoundness had but a sole difference from Pluto - satellites sent to the otherwise empty space with varoos sort of instruments analyzing whatever could and could not be detected. Nothing could be discovered.

The same happened when satellites were sent to explore the empty areas of Uranus, Saturn, Jupiter and mars. There were no moons, no rings -none of their original atmospheric conditions existed any longer.

Additionally, each had gone bye-bye exactly days apart. Earth's three hundred sixty-five and a quarter day is next ladies and gentlemen.

Covid 19 Zombies

It was a short war. The dead rising once examined were all determined to be had found to possess a Covid trace in the tissue. Furthermore, the former the former death certificates all had the same designated cause of death. Covid 19, added to one or more additional causes, lung decease being the most prevalent.

Once this factor discovered most medical government official cried out quietly, "How were we to even believe that zombified bodies would come from a virus. We never ever thought to examine the dead bodies of Covid for consequences."

This covid dead were exhumed, burned to ashes. The ashes dissolved in hydrochloric acid.

Covid Zombie arising negated. The next year 2026 there were unprecedented torrential rains. After a planet-wide nine-month draught came for 514 days consecutive torrential rains. There had been planet-wide over ten thousand, but below eleven thousand drownings...

There at the torrential raining were what had been termed as homeless trotters. One of those shelters housed only females. Most were of ill repute. Some were stationed due to abusive relationships. Some even had mental discrepancies. The particular one mentioned here had just furnished completing an eighty-thousand-dollar repair. It wasn't even a rubber roof but completed with felt and roofing cement.

The small holes in the cement walls supporting the train bridge above the homeless recuperative facility were made by the two flocks' small urban birds to house themselves.

When the rains poured down the [xxx] were confined inside their own graves dug by themselves. Few of the embryo in their eggs survived.

In Kabul, Afghanistan, Imbego smells, the she goat herd watcher carved for himself another small morsel the imported cow's milk cheese. Just a little piece from the corner of the block given to him by his friend and guest from London, England. The Kraft, logo and producers name still sat a top the larger piece left in the White Westinghouse refrigerator back in his three-bedroom flat. Lars the gift giver learned on a Lilli berry tree not thirty feet.

Lars's mother had sent him a care package from Philadelphia, Mississippi in the state. The cheese was expressly for Lars's old school chose whom Lars would abide with for six weeks' vacation from dilapidated, the largest passenger airlines. Lars just happened to be lactose intolerant.

The highest setting on the laboratories microscope now examined by Doctor Zest, the planet's leading pathologist on diseases causing death was examined by two other equally prominent doctors in biological diseases areas concluded one hundred percent of the captured [evians], penguins, ostriches, urban birds and others all were infected with myocarditis.

Various types of birds' nests were found abandoned of any flesh whatsoever. Feathers in arrowless bones and were all that were left. Three types of predatory marks were left on the carcasses remains. Spiders, ants and other every aviary feeding evidence were what showed. Upon further examinations on more than eighty percent of the mediatory teeth mark left on the remains were found to be left unbelievably except the proof existed showed the birds that were eaten by predators that were already dead. Rechecking those findings also revealed that all flesh eaters were not only dead but had contracted the Covid-19 virus.

Across all the planet these findings had become apart in various species. In Namibia, Senegal and Ghana the African countries under the control of the Dutch country Holland not only had animals been discovered eaten by dead insects and other dead animals with the virus but it here first found that people began to eat living animals. Teeth prints in skulls, ribs and other skeletal parts, Covid -19 was disseminated in all of the finding. Evidence alienated the consumers were already dead. Yet the eaters of living animals and rodents consuming as the cremated Zombies had.

Shortly, less than ninety-one hours later in other countries those same findings became crystal clear. This was now planetwide. Human remains were discovered in the U. S. A., Portugal, Argentina, Panama, Canada,

Greenland, Iceland, Chad, Egypt, Israel, Great Britain, Germany, Italy and many more countries.

Now the search was on. Anyone found with Covid-19 was now to as soon as discovered interest and burned live.

That law became the most enforced law ever. In just under a three year span. Covid no longer existed.

One Moment of Fame

Hey Yall! First, I'd like to tell you all how much I appreciate you paying your hard-earned money to come to see my show tonight.

How is no one ever associate rolls with gravy? I've never really tried it - cheese whiz. If anyone tells you to tell a tale, you really ought to put your foot in their ass.

After eating a full box of ex-lax I had a straight bourbon with Pabst Blue Ribbon Cheese. I gave them a toast. Here's mud in your eye.

McGruff

When almost seven hundred fifty-thousands of one million people in the city you've born and raised in turn their eyes and sections on you do just bring you down and all the rest of the people save for a couple hands full in number do not give as much as a thought of a dome. Then you'd better be ready for the battles of your time. That is what happened to me, and I was, am and always will be.

Now picture this told the ordinary citizen to the Chief of Detectives. The crack house you want sits on a small street, Colwyn. Colwyn's traffic by cars goes from west to east. One end of the block is route number 611. The opposite end is 13tl' street. The 711 end has an empty dirt lot directly viewing Colwyn. There are usually a few parked cars on that lot. You Park your stake out with video camera viewing the entire block of Colwyn. That gives you all the evidence of drug dealing. You'll get one month's worth of buyers and also the dealers and their sales. Hovertrain all of smoke houses the users attend, likewise all the sellers' hangouts and places of residence. Both groups makes, models, years of the cars license plates included.

In these house are on occasions, frequent occasions prostitution and forced human trafficking.

Here's the part where your job gets just a tad-bit difficult. You may need the public's opinion for the D. A. to prob himself up.

What you've been doing wrong and wrong for so long is not using the full arm of the law and all the laws against the dealers and buyers that you should've been. Only a couple of for instances are needed to get you on track. First is the charges you haven't been using. By the way you could've and you should've. Number one, use your labs properly. Dealers sell drugs, usually cut drugs. You've been charging with the transporting, sales, manufacturing, and possession of, let's just say cocaine. Do not!! forget to charge them with selling without a license. Do not forget to charge them on that one for each one and everyone of the items used in crack. The same for powder. Each charge they are to be arrested charged and tries for separately. NO convictions are to concurrently.

All convictions are to served separately. That's just one. Then do the same for every trick- those whores get paid for.

Further more one separate charge for each time a forced difference was forced to sell his self or, and herself. Every time on every profit making venture you enlist the treasury department to street, book, try and convict separately. [xxx] no charge found guilty will be served concurrently.

"Has the jury come to a decision? Yes your honor," comes back the reply from the foreperson. "What is the jury's decision?" come the second question. "Not guilty! On all forty charges of murder in the first degree." "Was the verdict of not guilty unanimous?" The third and last question. The reply "Yes! Your honor."

The three defendants laughed that night of their victory party. The party came due to one man. The man that gives the mafia under-boss actor for the Don who would be home in two more years. Had that man been allowed success to the Don before the Don gave orders for drug pickups and deliveries there would be no question the Don would have walked.

One odd thing to all but the fully knowledgeable would be that man who gave them their road to those victories being celebrated could by role not attend this party. The was highly light skinned negroid. He was never going to be connected therefore he was and always will be denied entrance to such offering made men only.

Months ago . . . Your only problem is you do not know how to make hits, tell the Feds you did it and \vin in court. So I will tell you how? His schooling the mob's under-boss right there in front of the acting mafia chieftain's home made the under-boss smile when he indicated a finger-point of approval.

If anyone chose to speculate one would speculate the acting chieftain really enjoyed his wife that night.

A Short Take on O. W's

War of the Worlds

In Russia it is approximately three a. m. while Cruizev was still asleep words come from his mouth. Tietranya, his wife had just a few seconds returned to newlyweds bed from but cocoa and whipped goats sweetened cream decided to respond to the pornographic movie, her husband and she had watched late last night. She awakened her husband. He now fully awake tired at first glance decipher to whom it was his wife of four days would awaken him and afterwards dial her cell phone. When the recipient of her cell phone finally [xxx] up he shortly become aware that he recognized the voice on the other end.

Svetlaia Islagizt, his now mother-in-law queried somewhat alarmed as to why the call. No doubt Jahoc her husband and his newly wed spouse's biological father's ear was in tow to the conversation. Jahoc almost totally kept a tight rein on his own life partner. Should you have been aware ofSvetlania's awesome [xxx] than easily comprehension could engulf you as to verdict for that judgement.

As quickly as Krufzev was why the call barely only almost started to plane the existence to reasoning why the ... He relaxed. Ketrania as non-verbally answering. Shutting down all woold be inquiries. He only [xxx] to remember a dream. A dream only moments [xxx] how [xxx].

Sunkrish Bala an average looking middle aged Bangladeshian divorcee smiled in her bed. She was complete of her contemplation. I can do better and decided her course or orchestration. When uncovered his softer had become so many times before in the pest thirty-eight years one month and one day rediscovered Sunkrish's we appetite. Her first two or three with her mate when the urge arouse, and he slumbered she crept. In that over eight hundred early mornings many and storage to her satisfied her salivated lusting.

Matthew Lentz, Senkrist's home mate truly lusted, in her, he longed for her every day near or apart from. Sunkrish know this. A lust took round in their third year of collaboration was that he would never love any other than her, thus her devotion. Add to the picture Matthew Lentz's personal bank account rested when they met somewhere in the bottom line of nine billion pounds.

Matthew awakened. Sunkrist sled up to cover his mouth. She had this not forgotten her twenty one creation of incontinence and [xxx] fill [xxx] ledged. Matthew as thousands of times prior gulped, delightedly.

Some Imagination or A Most Imperfect couple

"You're a fake!" Beth Lehem shouted, scolding at her husband. "You've gotten to be the famous police detective in history. You solved all two of the greatest crimes in the last score of years. Yet every time T.V., radio, Newspaper, magazines, and radio interview you, you quote some mythical crime solver from fictitious books and weekly television."

"I most certainly do not," her husband, E. G. Spike replied."

"One more thing. The game is afoot. Awww, lieutenant. Here's what happened. Do any of those sound familiar? 'Silence.' Well, those are only a few of your famous quotes. Oh! I apologize. Did I say that? Those quotes were yours?" Remembering, Beth somberly, quietly replied. "Yeah, I have used those words some. Great!" Beth replied. "Now, you see that you're a fake using fictional detectives narratives. Those are my own." E retorted. "My very own words that I made up to help spark my career and they work for me today. Try this on for size," says Beth. "I'll be back." Sounds familiar? Yeeeah, E. comes back with. "That was one of the best lines I made for when shows went commentary to push-up on one of their sponsors."

Beth kissed her husband took off her bra. Really wonderfully shaped nice tits beckoned E., so Beth took off her panties keeping an unnecessary argument out of their home, licked bottom lip wetly from left to right, touched her husband's private parts and [xxx] as a Jaybird slowly switched those tight, slightly rounded buttocks upstairs towards the bedroom.

Her husband E. did exactly the same.

WHILE IN THE [SPANSE] OF SUCKING TIME

I am one hundred percent accurate that most American adults have heard thc story of thc barbcquer being asked by his wife if the ribs are ready. The scene been in book, newspapers and movies, even some shorts. The answer while enjoying one of stock of well-done, tasty is usually "no".

It is only when one picks up a rib and all meat falls from the bone that the barbequer slight of pressure feels the de-mea ted bones marrow ooze into ones mouth from the two or four teeth that the cook has reason to be scolded if caught by the wife. During that momentary heaven of the delectable does his best friend, Fido come near the given tasty treat. Fido's recently born pups stand aside their pop their treats in [xxx] of tl1eir dad's. Now devoured tl1e need to wash down any remaining tender pieces that due to being well cooked have lost their crunch that their Mommsen's milk titillates them. When fully nourished their decision made while suckling to leave dad some of the flavor draws the dad to his fern ate. Two things await. Dad if smart and if worthy licks each and every one of those teets clean and more.

We all know what happens next.

EXEMPLAR

You are apt to set your molar tightly on the tiger's [anuspore]. You had best have the most desirable quality of running shoes. That will finish what you may start if you are unqualified. What you have the look of puts your palm to the hot irons.

Carry you are goodly amount of tomato juice and in hours the stretch may be quelled. You want to put down what may not be possible to put down and what knows it.

For this one I would advise you to put on a coat, but you threw yours away. When you look below you, you'll understand the floor is grievously rotted. Remember, a loose morals female may be avenged by other than her children's father's family. When close are your enemies diligence must not be stealthy. It was nice talking to you. Okay but while you lye there at rest I remind you now ahead of time. I told you so. In the event you never listen to me and head. You can hear me. This may be the lead in to that time I told you about. His reply to my exemplar - grease in the word.

DREAMS IN NIGHTMARE

Microft Learner is the Chief Physician at Ariola Hospital center city in Rodney East, Texas. He is speeding d1rough Plaster Street, Rodney's main trafficked drive following two police motorcycles.

His medical light flashing on the roof of his Chevrolet makes the pedestrian traffic well aware to keep clear of his movements or is the bleating blare of the motorcycles leading his way. Perhaps both. Oilier transports follow and parallel on side streets.

His thoughts- "I am finally going to make the evening news."

Two city blocks to their rear following are various autos. All the drivers are in their own personal vehicle. Mai Chasarwa, a surgical nurse usually thinks in Japanese, her pride, not for convenience's sake trusting some may comprehend the emergency awaiting her will keep her way somewhat clear.

Mainly, I going to be on T.V. is what occupies her inner most private thought.

Oh my God, that's a cute dress thought Doctor Prett A. Porte, best heart surgeon on the planet. He had a small problem on what to get Felicia Ashley Porte, his fashion conscious fourteen-year-old. Her fifteenth is in two days.

Fa, short for her first two names and oral prayer unknown to none except himself and Laura his wife with the perfect size thirty sixes that their daughter never becomes lesbian or bi is going to go crazy in school. She's going to sew me on television!

The story of the twenty-passenger corporate hears crashing in Rodney Texas hit some people in the New York, New York. Beth Shalom Mineral Cache Corporation with great joy. Our stocks are about to skyrocket. Their entire executive board died in that crash.

Samuel Joshua Dietz told all the board execs and the execs top staff to stay sharp in mind and appearance. We know who on top will be media interviewed. That we can control. The rest of you looks good for television. Give our stocks every reason to enrich our pockets and our shareholder.

I'm going to get my mom on T.V.

RESEARCH AND DEVELOPMENT

In the year twenty-one ninety-two the one hundred nine story high skyscraper on Mars Southwest gully for no apparent reason fully collapsed.

Only one living being survived. The apartment/condo complex was close to opacity in residents of home.

Evacuation began the night of the falling Among the thousands of dead bodies recovered there were listed mostly children at play or studying their school lessons. Most by vast majority the pets of which only 8 pet rats survived were discovered to have died with fed bellies. The dishes only had food or kibble in them.

Healthy young couple were unveiled in natural form. One way or another. Some were rich. Some were famous. A goodly number of them were rich and famous. Not surprisingly when more than one of the stories crushed some couples quickly as you should find the couples partial privates' dismemberments had shown their unawareness.

Margaret Thatcher, one of the top three television news reporters was found with two fingers in her part-time lovers backwards private part and tongue there also. She is mentioned here only because she had been wed less than two months. Her husband's guard unit was called-up just three days before the collapse.

Do You See Me Now?

An inquiry was injected to a police officer found guilty in a court of law. The verdict meated out twenty-two years behind bars convicted of murder while having his knee on the neck of his already apprehended and handcuffed prisoner on lying down the asphalted street directly close to the police officer's patrol car. The dead apprehended man's male sibling, possibly a stepbrother, I have not that articulating advice did verbally inquire of the convicted police officer, "What was going through your head when you had your knee on my brother's neck?"

The retort was not aired at that time, if ever.

I and I alone on my own and without permission allotted me gives this knowledgeable yet only speculated hypothesis, retort.

What was going through your mind when just prior to your brother's death that according to regulations. "I did attempt to put your brother in the squad car. Your brother resisted me putting him the rear of the car and he resisted verbally as much as physically insisting he make me aware of his claustrophobic medical condition? Had your brother not lied to me about his faked condition he would still be alive even unto this day?"

Further did the officer enlighten the sibling and all others in the courtroom. "What was going through your bead when you and your family knew that your new deceased brother was committing crimes passing counterfeit twenty-dollar bills accepting a big possibility of being caught, tried, convicted and sentenced to prison. What was going through your and your families head realizing should that have happened while he served his time behind bars that child molesters for decadenous decades have raped little children because the child's mother left that child with her live-in boyfriend? What was going through yours and your families head when some if not call of your profited from the passing of formerly passed counterfeit monies?"

"What is now going through your and your families' heads. Knowing should it your now deceased brother's family had turned him in he could have been apprehended peacefully and still be alive today?

This question I ask of His Honor the judge and this states prosecuting attorney, "What is going through your heads realizing all the crimes just mentioned in this courtroom by me in front of television cameras,"

It Works

Orlando Ricardo Garcia Picon, Carlita Picane Picon, wife and husband, Cannondo Ortiz and Gabriella Elista all a demised. The only survivor Rodrigo Ricard Picon, two months of age.

In the air balloon crash from one hundred feet, the question that loomed for six months now, "how did the infant survive," answered this morning.

Please [xxx] what appeared at first sight a horrific action by the child's father and mother at a further look shows the love of parents for their son.

Here we see seconds before the balloon crash claims the tree of the four allotted passenger [xxx] father [xxx] the [xxx] the bottom of the deflated aircraft and at the last seconds, the parents jump upward from the balloon's floor catching their baby while in the three are airborne, the flotation devices slams into the cement ground the child [xxx] the hard impact because the [xxx] or a half second after the aircraft, saving the infant from death.

A very short time passes as the news reporter gathers [xxx], then looking directly into the camera, states, mom, dan when, I go off air please answer your phone.

What's that Bump in the Middle of Your Body between Your Lower Spine and the top of Your thighs?

Doing the shows live airing, her thought through more than likely not meant to reach the audience. This morning, I fingered myself.

From a viewing paint in a private house came this thoughtful idea. She's got a job. It was followed with this helpful suggestion. Go downtown to the Convention Center, tell all the homeless guys you want dick, and you have a good job. Line them up around the building and start feeling the penises until you feel the one that suits you.

Ok, one other thin in case you go that other may when you seem satisfied feel under that shaft. If you find a slit under that cock, and at the bottom of the slit is a hole, you have found a hermaphrodite. Your freaky dick is now [xxx] covered.

Block

I am sitting here thinking on writing a short cop story. Chicago P. D. in my television set so notch my mind locks on the thought that perhaps it's influencing me.

I am about to laugh. The scene on the show is about to play out and before it shows I know exactly what is going to happen. Check me. See if I am wrong. I will lead you in up to the point I realized what would come on. If you do not figure it out before I write it, then you do not watch much tv.

The cops get a clue who needs to be questioned. The perpetrator they have figured out also has a job. The cops know where the perpetrator works. The cops go to the perp's job and ask another employee where the perps or the cops simply say to another employer the perps name that they are looking for. The asked employee usually knows the perm and points the pert out.

The perp, usually across some area a distance where it should be humanly impossible to hear that the cops are asking for him (usually him though not always) looks up towards the cops. The cops look the perp in the face. This little tit-bit ought to help confuse the issue. The cops are most often in plain clothe and no badges are exposed. The perp sees people talking in plain clothing remember -please excuse my written language?

And hauls ass! Takes it on the lamb, attempts to escape, makes a run for it, get's gone, high tales it etc., etc., etc.

WHY?

G - OR - G FOR YAWEE

Samuel Alloisciousu Tinatent Annen Nost, walked through all of the major churches owned and operated by The Archdiocese of Philadelphia, Pennsylvania in the Unites States of American. He had left his personal influences behind to attach itself to a soon to visit them by a most important person and his very important entourage.

There was one however who if he had had the power his warning to the Pope not to visit Philadelphia it is considered had most likely that the Pope would not have had to be explained why it seemed after the visit to Philadelphia about his same sex couple message given in Rome's neighboring country the Vatican City.

His warning was for Pope Saint Francis not to visit that most sinful city, he said, "do not visit Philadelphia. It will corrupt you." He also was a resident of that city.

That country's President had recently signed into law U. S. citizens now lawfully could same sex marry. The country's motto's: "In God We Trust; and One Nation Under God." The two mottos, "In God We Trust," has been on tlle country currency since July thirteenth, 1956. That was done by President Eisenhower.

What chewed his craw it that when the law was mandated on same sex marriage approval was that of all those God preaching television evangelist found the change in venue - not one adverse word. The Pope did not have a chance.

Fiction? Only Partly

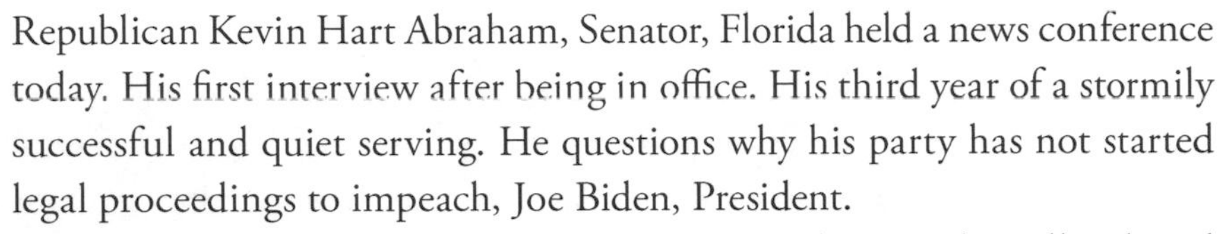

Republican Kevin Hart Abraham, Senator, Florida held a news conference today. His first interview after being in office. His third year of a stormily successful and quiet serving. He questions why his party has not started legal proceedings to impeach, Joe Biden, President.

His speech has shocked not only the United States, but all political parties planetwide.

The leading of the U. K., Russian, China, Germany, Japan, Brazil, Venezuela, Greece, Scotland, and twenty of the nations from Africa among others have all commented.

It is being looked into by the Federal Bureau of Investigation and the Department of the Treasury looking at what Abraham has alleged.

The report was that before being elected President and after having served as Vice President that Mister Biden was employed as C. E. O. of the then newly constructed Civic Center in Philadelphia that he (Biden) hardly ever if at showed to the Civic Center for work. If that was true and can be verified than now President Biden did commit federal crimes.

As when an entity is paid to do a job it is illegal not to do the job. Technically, it only has to be found out and proved that Biden was paid even one day for work that he did not do.

A point forthrightly brought out was that homeless people were sleeping on the sidewalks of the deca-million dollar newly constructed center for every day and night for almost three years while Biden served as C. E. 0. It was further elucidated in question, did Biden know of the homelessness on that property used for worldwide conventions.

"I must bring out, if Biden did know of the urine-soaked property visited by people from around Earth, why did he allow it. He either allegedly did not know, did not care of was incapable of being able to cease such a disparaging situation for three years.

Perhaps if true some will allow our President where a constituent of his ignominy rages.

If he cannot be impeached a committee of ascertaining the how nots and why nots I would not abhorrent to, if true!!!"

Over to Shenandoah Antebellum, with the weather.

GINGERS

The twin brothers had been at each other since they three years old, when Kyle, the older allowed Kile, the younger to be blamed for butter Kyle left on the kitchen floor overnight. Kimmee, their seven-year-old sister slipped on the melted greasy cobble stone floor the next morning and broke her right elbow socket. As soon as the cost came, she left booked both the twins.

The twins had been going at one another all month with furry. For all the years they never cause one another all physical pain. No one else in the family ever found out about their family feud. Mentally they had torn each other apart, but the hopper stone was they got mentally tougher.

Kile had an ant farm he was using as a scientific project. The boy as was his brother a genius among the geniuses of his age group. The movie about the superhero scientist got into brain a couple of years back and along with his other ventures he determined it could be done. The controlling of living ants was his most dedicated to his time.

Kyle knowing Kile well said to him, "I will find out which of those ants is your favorite, favorite being equivalent to the test subject progeny.

Kile knew Kyle as well as Kyle knew Kile, sort of believed that should he ever make the step forward his brother thought that he already had, his experiments and his time would be killed thusly his dream the one ting his brother Kyle did not know of his becoming a real-life superhero's annihilation would commence. That on the backburner only because his achievement had not come to fruity. That self-same day while on his Mac computer the answer popped.

DID I TRIUMPH?

I desired to script a shorter story fascinating essentially eighty percent upper-level location to insulate an avant-garde Mister Howard Cosell. My grail was for fountain heads with firsthand awareness who have read my works and also instruct the soon to postulate grand education, the two, three, four and five Gaussian years old, offspring a true lexicon ameliorated road to show off without unfluctuating vociferation.

Conservation Genetics NASA Division

It's Balmy Out (I. B. O.) covered up Doctor Seazi Deen's disappearancc via the means of faking her demise. Her sons and daughter were the only small concerns to complete secrecy. ·what they were not privy to was her husband Rodney Paul Deen's mental acuity her had amusingly developed by way of sexually attending his wife in the last thirty nine years. Seazi, did not know of their connection either. He had kept it secret since he attended the ability. There was no marriage sexual infidelity among her peers and among her social association. In some instances, he chose exactly right. She had become more than attracted to over ten men and extremely interested in her boss Helen Reddy. To date he had managed to demolish all their attentions. He acquired that insight to her mind and vision through her own eyes twenty-nine earlier.

NOT VERY PROMISING

He had finally made it. Twenty movies Ten weekly television shows and four ideas sold to the two most published authors over the past thirty years. Those aside he was now more popular on the internet than the next thirteen writers downloaded. In all totaled one billion six hundred thousand in the black.

Locus lowest and on the billionaires list. You millionaires can go fuck yourselves.

NOT VERY PROMISING

His very thought at seventy years of age his next thought I'll probably never get to say that to you billionaire, head faced to the floor, tilted, his left eye squinted upwards, that expression on his purposely come what worked-smirks on his face leaded only to allow questioning should one wish to decipher what he had in his mind. Consternation leading only to unknowing frustration.

A genuine genius his ingenuity flowed on every article mixing truth, historical truth in along side of true intellectual imagination forced his standed head-over-heels above each contemporary daring to affix their own above standard accomplishment. None come within a shout of his own align men. The ex-love of his life was the most recent would-be contender barely even advanced to flapdoodle.

When asked about his wife's latest writings, he gave but one one-word reply, "Claptrap".

The Juanita Kidd Stout Warning

Jackson!! I'm gonna kill!! I'm gonna kill!! I'm gonna you!! Vehemently Geddesh was screaming as loudly as she could. If her lungs could possibly contain more air her Jackson outbursts could come through the thick steel doors the Sheriff's officers just closed and are now with force returning her to the holding cell. Still, she extolls.

I'm gonna kill you, Jackson! Jackson!! Jackson!!!! Jackson!!!

Back in the holding cell with the other prisoners either awaiting their turn to see the judge or already having seen the judge and being returned to prison those awaiting return exchange their story and allowing the others to know what amount of time the judge sentenced them to serve behind locked doors and secured prison walls.

Calm now, she tells of her crime of stabbing her mother and her own boy friend after returning home from work. Opening her door, she was alarmed to find her mother copulating with the soon to be son-in-law. She stabbed him too. They were doing the eighty-eight-position naked as the J-bird.

She farther related that the said she almost had the right to be given a not guilty sentence because it was a possibility taking in account the victims relationship to her that a temporarily vicinity may have overtaken her. He thirty-five-year sentence which came along with the guilty verdict is the maximum she could receive was handed down only because the Judge had to take into account that the butcher [night] knife used to stab and slice the surviving couple was taken from the accused purse which was brought in the home with her.

Leaving the courthouse Bezo Arlett, the sliced and stabbed fiance of the convicted woman said "Eileen Breastben, the convicted woman's mother, [hispette], referring to the jailed woman, really lost it. She kept calling me Jackson Eileen, with no sense of what was about to happen," said to him, Jackson is only a slang term for mother-fucker.

The two went to his apartment and did the full trip around The World, over and over and over.

Finally, This is an Ending

The Arena a usual for an affair of such a skeptical of show business had been publicized as sold out weeks ago. One or two single seats did remain. The building opened on time. Most of the leather chairs were filled. A few groups owning them for this show were still lollygagging in the vast Jobby and some attaining the upper seating ascending the main, east and west stairways.

The vestibule by the larger of rl1e two men's room attendant having only moments ago returned to his duty. The middle-aged couple he had passed off the heroin packet to sniff the small chunky substance.

One man still not entering because he was deciding which of the remaining single seats he would choose.

The loud speaking came no. There was no static. The announcement only reported itself once. Each time lasted only a moment to a minute. Tonight's show is canceled due to injury of the performer.

The crowd pissed off as hell had just started to verbalize their complaints. The Arena, fell to pieces from the size of dust particles to those of approximately two to three feet.

Forty-eight thousand patrons died.

Sixteen years later The Arena's return opening is scheduled for tomorrow night eight fifteen p.m.

The bomber has not been caught nor has the bomber's identification been ascertained.

Four Eyes

He found his wife has had and still does have two lovers on the side. Hoping to renew his romance with her, he paid Federal Express delivery company to deliver his wife a gift. The gift was to be delivered just prior to her leaving for work in the morning, as it was.

He knew since she was not expecting anything her curiosity naturally would have her right away open the box as she did.

Normally she would have pulled her car to the side, park it and have her rendezvous then go her merry way to her place of employment.

In her kitchen attaining a six in steak knife she opened the box, sat down and stayed home.

History

Just a short blur to correct what has been taught as true history. Here is a name. See if you know the reason it is written here before I tell you why I write this name is history that should not be denied?

Moses Fleetwood Waker.

PRESSURE

Since the fall semester of my first year CCP I had decided on being a writer. The city that raised from birth this talented scriptist had other plans. Overall, most of townships people had me pegged to be an actor. I found actors and minstrels of success mind you netted somewhere in the area of the salaries. Writers of those super hits weather play or vocalization outdistanced those upfront appearing before their evidence monetarily by far. Kept a major part of their privacy.

Being home for family affair positive and negative overshadowed them and the upper elitist classes showered writers with aplomb more rigorously. Performing to authoring -sucks nard.

Not such an undistinguished lead into telling you my own personal reason for not patting me on my back with elated sounds due to my pride in my style of writing. You see I have since I started putting my ideas on paper considered the formatting solely my own cognition. Imagine my enlightenment after downloading and concentrating to old-time radio. Dang that Alan Ladd and Russell Hughes working together.

Still my ideas you read are provocatively fresh and in-the-main my own.

Therefore, I lay claim to its fancy creative power.

Read On.

Seventy-Five Percenters Part One

The troop of Yugoslavian nationals all followers of their now legendary table tennis team got into an impromptu bar discussion. Discussion once again a soft heavy breathing vehicle to comradery

The finals leading to Western Hemisphere Championship tomorrow afternoon. Here because the first match of the year Constantinople lost. Lost is a under rated word. The scores for every Yugoslavia proved Constantinople may as well not had made the trip. The two teams met once in the opening rover of the tournament Yugoslavia's record to get to the tournament was fifty-eight wins twenty-nine losses. The same outcome as their first match is why the extolling of legendary was rang around the tennis table world.

A loss in the first round meant pack your bags the trip is over. Before housing to access the round trip, jet airline tickets Constantinople's wins were seventy-nine losses, uh, uhh loss, one.

The final is to be between Brazil vs. Uganda and Yugoslavia vs China.

The now quieted scene argument was between China, Brazil and Yugoslavia, Uganda consciously was due to their close loss by only one point to Yugoslavia in their regular season. Strategy and rest were on the agenda's plan to win. The team's manager and coaches looked forward to future employment. Skipping the revils was a great idea if it works

COSB'S WISDOM?

Then how the hell did women have babies? Want the last sentence and the beer stein landed. Hardly? The head it landed on had no hat, so as the launched downward and simultaneously forward the gash appeared. Then shortly like a river flowed the crimson.

That's the way I would have liked to pen part two. It just collided against the calm of part one.

From this day fourth you shall bare your children in pain. Did you understand the phrase? From this day fourth. Man being the jackass as he is deciding to give you birthers pain blockers in direct violation of a Holy decree.

Honorary Doctor William Henry Cosby Junior had a different decisional idea. Quote Kiss and blah the baby appears. Remember that one? If not further elaboration -if like 'em, you dip 'em into the lacquer. Cause if you don't dip in the lacquer, they'll fade on you.

I heard to on one of his albums when I was eleven or twelve years old. I'm sixty-seven years old now. Till this day I did not realize the depth of wisdom in those few lines when put together.

God's and Cosby's.

From this day forth. That spot little ones come forth into this world had to cause pain by own decree. Stated earlier, I was not here at that time. If not for pain blockers called saddle blocks women hurt when children come out. Kiss em? Leads me to this question, where did they come from and did not hurt before from this day forth?

EXISTENCE

Logerfield is a classic land developer. His contract with, Smithfield, Alan and Ellen Incorporation is a very profitable one. Perhaps it is thee most important in Logerfield's history of existence.

Matenware is a large as S. A. and E and gave Logerfield another huge contract. The only catch is until Matenware releases Hesychius and Plush from its contract Logerfield is not allowed on Matenware's old properties which need refurbishing.

Citizenwide Logerfield is viewed as the only up and coming high-riser. The people praise the surge Logerfield is making. All but Alloishus Keliant who has partnered with Blessed George the privately owned corporation that beat out Logerfield for the Homecheck project a lifelong renewable source of revenue. Blessed George is owned and chaired by family of Bendover N. Smile & rival to the [xxxxx] love of the stepson of the owner of Logerfield. His first name is a weird one, Danger. The son has basically lend his hatred side of the home developed personality towards all but his mother's living partner.

Business and family mixes very, very well in today's times of foolhardiness.

Everything was looking for like peaches and cream and champagne dreams.

The Sun where all planets and moons used to held in place by various degrees of its gravity's pull exploded.

To Extreme to Bear

Business and family mixes very, very well in today's times of foolhardiness.

Everything was looking for like peaches and cream and champagne dreams.

The sun where all planets and moons used to hold in place by various degree of its gravity's poll exploded.

To Extreme to Bear

Mix O'barren the Irishman answering the incoming calls at the news desk at WRJKX-TV News after his thoughts settled from his last call began to calm his attitude by calling on his past reserve. He had at one time in the post hung up on that very some caller. Since that time the caller had called a few more times with some somewhat honest opinions on present day his that gave O'barren cause to pause for thought.

This particular time caused him to not only see red but though he kept his mouth shut he was for a short time overheated with short temper.

In the U.S. A., Philadelphia, Pennsylvania to be exact there were citizens crying, pleading begging actually to there nosy or to stop the gun small number of gun death plaguing the city the past year and a half. This occurred shortly after the city rioted breaking into stores and business loating and destroying other people's properties because a black guy was taking a chances on going to jail for passing counterfeit twenty dollar bills taking the chance that white being imprisoned if found guilty by the legal system of his young daughter being physically abused and sexually molested by her mothers new guy either having continual sex with the child's mother not living in the females abode or living the child's mother residential space.

Instead of going to jail the counterfeiter was killed by a Caucasian police officer. This the rioting Black Lives Matters, made a big show of themselves possible a fair to publicize themselves.

The report causing O'barron some heat was over two police officers during the ongoing period of the citizening begging to gave help them get safe from street killing's shot a man to death because during a large street gathering massive fights broke out. A gunman pulled a gun. The above police [xxxtion] accrued.

No Protest! No riots!!

The caller said not asked of O'barron, do you think he dead a gunman was a Caucasian? I do not hear any protest. I do not know of any riots. That's why I asked if he was a Caucasian. Maybe his life doesn't matter. Think. The caller further elaborated. If the gunman was black, no one carrying any placards, "Police Murder." No one displaying racial inequality signs. No riots.

No "black lives matter" signs. No Black Lives Matter, organization. No protest honoring a thief who put his children in danger. The thing stated by the caller, was the question "are you going to go out protest?"

O'barron finally thought, Insufferable.

The Shape of Matters

W'hen Gentet Abituli, the wife and mother of Prince Vliblet Abitoli was ask for a quick interview by her personal publicist she consented by answering in a code. One she had made on her own so she could complain and only her two teenager sons Mbuto, fourteen and Ojake, seventeen would be aware of what she was reminding them each to so something about. She and they knew the two must attend to their intelligence [as) to get it done but keep it convert.

He reply was sure, anything for you Tetstmet, albeit. Ableit is Gentot's favorite word in her dialogue, it must be only a few minutes, I am running a little behind.

About the Author

My history is in my books, so to all you other authors try this on for size.

I take imaginative liberty.

My mom was Venusian Princess. One of her parents four princesses. Oh and there was one uncle too.

My mom was their step-sister.

My dad, a dethroned King. Devoid of family, friends and fortune. I guess my mom took pity on him, so here I am.

Try that on for size.

Mr. Rodney Paul Williams
a.k.a
Rodney Paul Banks

Printed in the United States
by Baker & Taylor Publisher Services